STUNT
BUNNY

WITHDRAWN

First published in Great Britain in 2011 by Simon and Schuster UK Ltd,
a CBS company.

Text copyright © 2011 Tamsyn Murray
Cover and interior illustrations copyright © 2011 Lee Wildish

Simon & Schuster UK Ltd
1st Floor, 222 Gray's Inn Road, London WC1X 8HB

This book is a work of fiction. Names, characters, places and incidents are either the product
of the author's imagination or are used fictitiously. Any resemblance to actual people living
or dead, events or locales is entirely coincidental.

A CIP catalogue record for this book is available from the British Library.

978-1-84738-728-8

1 3 5 7 9 10 8 6 4 2

Printed and bound in Great Britain.

www.simonandschuster.co.uk

www.tamsynmurray.co.uk

STUNT
BUNNY

TOUR
TROUBLES

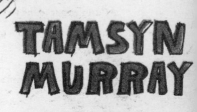

TAMSYN
MURRAY

ILLUSTRATED BY
LEE WILDISH

For Lily Slater, the naughtiest puppy ever.
Please stop eating the sofa.

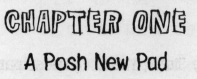

CHAPTER ONE
A Posh New Pad

It's not easy being Britain's best-loved bunny. If I'm not meeting my adoring fans or rehearsing my latest dare-devil stunt, then I'm being the darling of Saturday night TV on *Superpets*, the show where animals are the stars. Some people think my life is all chomping on carrots and waggling my powder-puff tail, but there's a lot more to it than that. Trust me, being *this* cute is hard work.

Not that I get any special treatment for being bigger than Bugs Bunny. My owner, Susie, understands what a celebrity pet needs. She's pretty clever for an eight year old and is always ready with a perfectly prepared popcorn stick, but the rest of the Wilson family are a bit clueless. Mrs Wilson does her best, but Susie's little sister, Lily, once tried to marry me to the family cat, Smudge. And don't even talk to me about Susie's dad, the man who makes Captain Hook look friendly. I don't know why he's got

6

it in for me. Maybe he's secretly jealous because no-one wears T-shirts with *his* face on.

Anyway, it's thanks to him that my hutch is practically falling down around my ears and all because he's too mean to buy a new one.

I call him EE, which stands for Evil Edward, and the name suits him perfectly. I mean, everyone knows a celeb should live in a posh pad with a diamond encrusted water bottle and fresh hay cut by their own butler, right? 'I don't know what all the fuss is about,' he said when Susie pointed out the flaking paintwork and rusty bars on my tatty old door. 'Where's my screwdriver? I'll have it fixed in no time.'

I didn't like the sound of that. EE might think he was a Do-It-Yourself whizz, but anything he tried to fix ended up being

Destroy-It-Yourself. There was no way I was letting him loose on my hutch. Luckily, it seemed Susie felt the same way. 'The vet says Harriet has grown. She needs a bigger house.'

'Nonsense,' EE replied, slapping his hand on the top of the hutch and making the walls wobble. 'This one is fine.'

Susie looked very determined. 'There's one on special offer at the pet shop.'

A-ha! Now this was more like it. I knew exactly which one she meant –Mulberry Mansion. It had two floors, a bathroom and a paddling pool for those hot summer evenings. A hutch like that was so much more *me* and now it was within my reach. All I had to do was convince EE and I knew exactly how to do it.

With one carefully placed back leg, I kicked hard at the side of the hutch. There was a creak as the wooden wall peeled away and landed with a thump on the grass. For a second, I didn't move. Then I was off, zooming towards EE's prize-winning roses. I hadn't actually planned to eat them, but now that I was close enough to smell them, I couldn't resist a nibble.

'Get away from my flowers!' EE shouted, running towards me and waving his arms. 'Susie, wait for me in the car. As soon as I've caught that pesky rabbit, we're going to the pet shop.'

I let myself be bundled into my travelling basket to wait whilst they went to collect my new home. At last, I thought, a plush pad I could invite my famous friends to. Maybe EE wasn't so bad after all.

Of course, I should have known something would go wrong. But it wasn't until EE had finished putting the new hutch together and the whole family gathered around to inspect it that the full horror dawned.

'Ta-da!' He waved a proud hand at my new home.

I stared. Never mind the wonky legs and upside down door, instead of a super-deluxe Mulberry Mansion, I was looking at a Cosy Cottage. It wasn't even a rabbit hutch. The torn packaging on the ground clearly read 'Gerbil House'.

Lily stopped chewing Barbie's hair and pushed the soggy doll towards the open cage door. 'Just right for my dolly.'

'I'm sorry, Harriet,' Susie said sadly.

'Mulberry Mansion was sold out. This was all they had left.'

Mrs Wilson looked doubtful. 'It's a bit small.'

EE didn't seem sorry at all. 'Rubbish. It's *cosy*, that's all. She'll soon get used to it.'

Smudge flicked his tail smugly and padded indoors to his roomy, fur-lined cat bed. Grinding my teeth, I hopped inside and immediately bumped my nose on the back wall. EE sniggered, then turned it into a cough when Susie glared at him. If I didn't know better I'd say EE enjoyed moving me into a Z-list hutch. Maybe now you see why I call him Evil Edward.

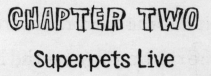

CHAPTER TWO
Superpets Live

The way I won my place on the *Superpets* TV show is the stuff of legend. From the moment TV presenter Gloria Goodwood saw me pull off a perfect bunny backflip at our church village fair, I've never looked back. She invited me to take part in the *Superpets*

Search for a Superstar and, after a gruelling audition process, the public voted me the winner and my life changed forever. I was no longer a boring pet bunny, I was Harriet Houdini: Stunt Bunny! And, just like every other star, I had my share of crazy fans, like the Great Maldini, who tried to kidnap me for his magic act.

During the auditions I'd made some great friends, like Cherry the counting kitten and Lulu the hula-hooping chimp. Unfortunately, I'd made a couple of enemies too – Doodle the opera-singing poodle and her owner, Miranda. They thought they were better than all the other contestants. So, when I scooped first place in the final and Doodle and Miranda stormed off the stage in a huff, I didn't mind. In fact, I didn't care if I never saw them again. And I might not have done, if Gloria hadn't come up with a little surprise to keep us busy when *Superpets* had a month long Easter break from filming.

'Ah, Mr Wilson, I'm glad I caught you,' she said, bustling over to EE as he cleared my dressing table up after we'd finished the last show. 'Do you have time for a quick chat?'

Now, it's no secret in the Wilson household that EE goes a bit funny when Gloria is around. His cheeks turn pink, a big, goofy smile crosses his face and his tongue gets tied up in knots. Mrs Wilson says sniffily that he's got 'a thing' about Gloria Goodwood. I don't know about that, but it does make him look very odd.

'Grnf,' he said, nodding his head up and down. 'Defsolutely.'

Gloria's smile slipped a little bit. 'Er – good. Well, I've got some exciting news. We're taking Superpets on the road in a special tour called *Superpets Live* and we'd love Harriet to take part. She's bound to be the star of the show!'

My ears stood on end as I imagined my name at the top of the posters. I liked the idea of being the headline act! And the more time I spent away from cramped Cosy Cottage, the better. I'd have to persuade Smudge to do some damage whilst I was away – he needed a new scratching post, maybe he could use the legs of my hutch . . .

'I was thinking of six or seven dates over two weeks,' Gloria went on. 'We'll be staying at the best hotels, of course, and you'll both be well looked after.'

I twitched my whiskers in irritation. What did she mean, 'both'? If she thought I was spending a whole two weeks on my own with EE, she had another thing coming! It wasn't as though he even did anything interesting – his idea of fun was snoozing in front of the snooker on TV with a cup of cocoa. No, if we were going on tour, Susie *had* to come with us.

But EE's face lit up and I knew he was imagining himself staying in a luxury

21

hotel. He coughed. 'That sounds nery vice, Miss Goodwood.'

'Oh, please,' Gloria said, patting his arm. 'Call me Gloria.'

EE's cheeks turned even pinker. 'Will it be just us on the tour, G-Gloria?'

Gloria smiled. 'Oh, no, there'll be lots of other pets from the show and the auditions.' She looked at the clipboard in her hand. 'Let's see, we have Cherry the counting kitten, Trevor's terrific tumbling terrapins, Lulu the chimp and Spike-tacular, the hedgehog dance group. Oh, and Doodle the opera- singing poodle. You remember her, don't you?'

The last time I'd seen Doodle, she'd

been up to her snooty nose in pond water and very unhappy with me. It was a memory that had cheered up many a boring hour in my bunny hutch, but  I wasn't jumping for joy that she'd be on the tour too. If I knew Doodle and her owner Miranda, they'd be looking for a way to get their own back on me.

'It sounds great.' EE was beaming at Gloria. 'I'll book the time off work. Just name the date and we'll be there!'

He was right, I decided after they'd sorted out all the details and EE was carrying me back to the car; it did sound great. The only real problem was Doodle. What dirty tricks would she and Miranda have up their sleeves this time?

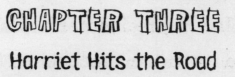

CHAPTER THREE
Harriet Hits the Road

It wasn't until we got home and EE spilled the beans about *Superpets Live* that I realised he really wasn't planning to take Susie. Great, I was going to be stuck with him after all. Susie didn't look very happy either.

'But who will tuck Harriet in at night

and read her a story?' she asked, her blue eyes filling with tears and her bottom lip starting to wobble.

EE threw me a brisk look. 'I'm sure Harriet will be far too busy practising her backflips to need a bedtime story.'

Folding her arms, Susie said, 'Of course she'll want a story. And she needs lots of toys and her special fluffy blanket too.'

Susie was too well behaved to stamp her foot, but I wasn't. I thumped hard on the living room floor to make sure everyone knew I was not a happy bunny.

'I don't see why she can't go with you,' Mrs Wilson said, smiling at Susie. 'It is the school holidays, after all, and I'm sure there'll be plenty of room on the tour bus.'

'Luxury coach, actually,' EE said, his expression turning dreamy. 'Gloria said it's got a TV and a coffee machine and everything. No expense spared, according to Gloria.'

Raising an eyebrow, Mrs Wilson said, 'Oh, I expect you and Gloria are going to have a wonderful time.'

Even I could hear the warning in Mrs Wilson's voice, but EE seemed to have missed it completely. 'I think you're right. Gloria says she's going to take very good care of me.'

He wandered off, whistling the *Superpets* theme tune. Mrs Wilson watched him go, hands on hips. 'That settles it, Susie, you're going on that tour.' she said, shaking her head. 'Someone has to keep an eye on your dad. He's gone Gloria ga-ga.'

Worse than that, I decided with a cross twitch of my whiskers, he'd completely forgotten who the star of the show was. At some point, I'd have to remind him that he was just my roadie, but right now I had more important things on my mind. With only a few days before we went off on tour, I had packing to do. Two weeks away from home was a long time.

✹ ✹ ✹

On Monday morning, EE made a ridiculous fuss when he saw the amount of luggage I had. 'Seven bags?' he exclaimed, staring at the matching cases Susie had piled up by the front door. 'She's only a little rabbit. What on earth does she need seven bags for?'

I suppose it was hard for him to understand – when he's not at work he slobs around the house in scruffy jeans and a saggy old cardigan – but I have an image to maintain. What would my fans think if I went out on stage looking less than my best?

Susie ignored him and peered into my travel basket, her face scrunched up anxiously. 'Are you going to be alright in there, Harriet?'

'I'm sure she'll be fine,' soothed Mrs Wilson.

'But Dad says I'm not allowed to let her out on the bus and it's such a long way to Glasgow.' Susie looked from one parent to the other. 'What if she needs a wee?'

'We'll put some sawdust in there,' EE said firmly. 'There's no way I'm risking another rabbit rumpus.'

He glared down at me and I knew he was thinking of the time I'd gone exploring on the train to my first *Superpets* audition. It had been his fault. Honestly, I don't know what he'd expected after he stuffed my basket under that smelly old seat.

Mrs Wilson gave Susie a big hug and planted a sloppy kiss on her nose. 'Bye bye, Susie. Be good.'

Lily watched and then turned to me.

'Bye bye, Hawwit,' she said in a stern voice, pushing her stubby fingers into the basket and almost poking me in the eye. 'Be good.'

Huh, that was a blooming cheek: Lily was the naughtiest little girl I knew. Even so, I was going to miss her while I was away, and Susie's mum too, but someone had to stay at home with Smudge. He was scowling at me sulkily

from under the hallway table and I knew he wished he was the one going on tour.

The doorbell made all of us jump a few seconds later. Glancing through the bobbled glass of the front door, I could just make out the *Superpets Live* banner on the side of the bus outside.

'Ready for an adventure, Harriet?' Susie whispered, picking up my basket.

A shiver of excitement ran through me as we climbed on board the bus, with Lily and Mrs Wilson waving us off. OK, so I was going to miss home and I had to put up with an overload of EE for the next two weeks, but I was going to be in the spotlight, doing what I loved best with Susie at my side. What could possibly go wrong?

CHAPTER FOUR

Are We Nearly There Yet?

I don't know about you, but I'm not a big fan of long journeys. There's no room to stretch your legs, Eye Spy gets really boring after the first hundred miles or so and it's only a matter of time until someone is sick. And when you're sat next to a kitten who insists on counting every single lamp-post all the way to Glasgow, those miles really drag. Don't get me wrong, I really like Cherry, but she has a passion for numbers and wants the world to know it.

You might think that EE would have wanted to sit beside me on the bus – after all, I was the reason he was there – but he couldn't wait to snap the specially made seatbelt around my basket.

'Sorry about this, Harriet. Gloria said the pets have to stay in their cages,' he said, taking a long, hard look around me to make sure I couldn't escape. 'We'll be in the owner's lounge at the back of the bus if you need us. Come on, Susie.'

Patting my cage, Susie said, 'It's only for a few hours, Harriet.'

Huh, I thought as they headed off towards a big TV screen surrounded by comfy looking seats, EE didn't sound sorry. In fact, he sounded pretty pleased about it. But at least I wasn't next to Doodle. Her owner, Miranda, had shuddered when she'd seen me.

'Ugh, we don't want you anywhere near that revolting rabbit, do we, Doodle?' she exclaimed and made sure she put the poodle as far from me as possible.

I didn't mind. Even though Doodle was safely strapped in, she didn't stop growling at me and I knew she'd aim a nasty nip my way if she got the chance. I could almost feel her evil stare drilling into me as we started on our way to Glasgow.

But it wasn't long before Doodle's growls turned whimpers. Only a few miles later, she was covering her eyes with her paws and making so much noise that the whole bus could hear her.

'What's that terrible racket?' EE asked, turning around to frown in our direction. 'I can't hear the television.'

'It's not Harriet,' Susie said, before EE could blame me. 'She's too small to make so much noise.'

Sam, the nine-year-old owner of Spike-tacular, put his fingers in his ears. 'Is that Doodle? She's not supposed to perform until she's on stage.'

'Don't be ridiculous,' Miranda snapped, jumping to her feet and hurrying towards us. 'My Doodle has a delicate tummy. Obviously, being on the bus doesn't agree with her.'

'Does she have to sing about it?' asked

Sam, as Doodle's howls got louder.

I wrapped my ears around my head, hoping they would drown out the noise, but Doodle was determined to make sure that everyone knew she was ill.

Miranda bent down, fussing around the cage. 'Is my Doody-Woody feeling sicky-wick?'

I don't know about Doodle, but Miranda's silly voice was enough to make *anyone* feel sick.

'Stop the bus!' Miranda demanded. 'Doodle *must* have some fresh air.'

'I can't stop on the motorway,' the

driver called back. 'But it's not far to the next service station. We can pull in there if you like?'

Doodle yowled miserably and Miranda fussed over her. 'We don't have much choice. Hang on, darling.'

Now, I'm no doctor, but even I could see that Doodle was suffering. Her nose was pressed flat against her seat and her eyes were squeezed shut. She didn't stop her pitiful moaning for a second. I could see what Sam meant; it did sound like she was singing, in a really awful, out of tune kind of way.

'Here we are,' shouted the driver, steering the bus off the straight motorway and around the bendy road to the service station. We all swayed. I glanced over at Doodle, who was now *very* green, and shuffled back inside my basket as fast as I could. Any minute now, she was going to blow and I didn't want to be caught in the crossfire.

'Oh, well done, Doody-Woody,' Miranda said, unfastening Doodle's harness as we stopped. She wrapped her arms around the dog in a big cuddle. 'We'll soon have you feeling much bet—'

There was a revolting retching sound from Doodle. Miranda let out a horrified wail and I clasped a paw to my nose as the smell of sick wafted

through the bus. Slowly, Miranda stood up. A blob of half chewed carrot plopped from her hair and on to her shoes.

'Urgh,' said EE, wrinkling his nose in disgust when he saw Miranda. 'Guess who won't be in the owner's lounge for the rest of the journey?'

Miranda tugged a wretched-looking Doodle towards the door. 'That suits me fine. I've never met a more boring bunch anyway.'

The two of them swept down the steps and off the bus. For a moment no one spoke, then EE turned to Susie. 'Do you know, it couldn't happen to a nicer couple.'

And for once, I actually agreed with him.

CHAPTER FIVE

I'm Ready For My Close-Up

I don't mind admitting that I've got expensive tastes. So, when the tour bus pulled up outside our hotel in Glasgow, I was keen to see what kind of luxury Gloria had in store for us. And I wasn't disappointed. Judging from the glittering lights around the gold entrance, the classy red carpet and the smartly dressed doorman, the *Landmark Hotel* was the poshest of the posh.

'Wow!' Susie said, her nose pushed up against the window of the bus. 'It's like something out of a movie.'

She wasn't wrong. The Landmark was clearly where all the stars came to stay, because huddled outside was a row of photographers, cameras in hand as they waited patiently to snap any visiting celebrities. As Susie clipped on my glittery black and silver harness and lead, I shook out my gorgeous grey fur and straightened up my whiskers. I was determined to look my best for the paparazzi. If it was a star they were looking for, they'd come to the right place.

From the moment we stepped off the bus, the cameras were flashing in our direction.

'Look, it's Harriet Houdini!' one called, clicking away furiously.

'Over 'ere, Stunt Bunny!' another shouted as he elbowed the photographer beside him out of the way.

'Give us a backflip!' a third cried, throwing himself on to the floor to get the best shot.

Susie and I turned towards them and I twitched my nose in the cutest possible way while they snapped away. EE hung around behind us, desperate to get into the pictures, but the photographers kept moving to cut him out.

'Oi!' one yelled, when EE gave up hovering in the background and thrust his grinning face up to mine. 'Do you mind? It's Harriet's mug shot we want, not yours.'

Then, Gloria appeared beside us. 'That's enough for now, gentlemen,' she said, ushering us towards the brightly lit revolving doors and waving a wagging finger at the photographers. 'If you want to see more of the sensational Stunt Bunny, you'll have to buy a ticket for tomorrow night's show!'

Grumbling, the paparazzi turned their cameras expectantly towards the bus, waiting for the next passenger to emerge from the narrow doorway. When Doodle and Miranda appeared, there was an excited burst of flashing lights. But, after the incident on the bus, neither of them was exactly looking their best.

Doodle's fur was flat and her eyes were dull. Miranda looked even worse and she held up one hand in front of her face.

Gloria hurried towards them and looked them up and down, before leaning closer. 'I wonder if you'd be better off using the entrance at the back of the hotel?' she murmured. 'We don't want any unflattering pictures of Doodle in the newspapers, now, do we?'

With a sulky scowl, Miranda led Doodle away. Seconds later, the paparazzi were snapping away at Cherry and Lulu. I almost felt bad for Doodle. Then I remembered how she and Miranda had tried to stop me from getting to the *Superpets Search for a Superstar* semi-final and, suddenly, I didn't feel so sorry for her anymore.

Once we were all off the bus Gloria gathered us all together beside the grand staircase in the centre of the hotel lobby.

'Welcome to the *Landmark Hotel*, your home for the next two nights,' she said, as her assistant checked a clipboard and handed out room keys. 'In the morning, we'll explain exactly what will happen on the tour. But tonight, feel free to enjoy everything this five star hotel has to offer.'

Sam's eyes were as big as Frisbees as he stared at the staircase. 'Imagine sliding down that.'

It looked like fun, but my attention was

fixed on Gloria as she described the
deluxe Jacuzzi and the rooftop terrace
bar, where the rich and famous came to
party. I pictured me and Susie making
friends with pop pin-ups and movie stars.

This was it, I realised, once Gloria had finished talking and a bell-boy was showing us to our room. This was what they called the Big Time!

CHAPTER SIX

What Happens on Tour, Stays on Tour

I don't know what happened when we got to our room. One minute I was backflipping from one bouncy double bed to another and 'accidentally' knocking over EE's signed photo of Gloria. The next, I was fast asleep and dreaming about meeting up with

Mickey and Minnie Mouse in the hotel bar and before I knew it, the sun was peeping through the curtains and Susie was shaking me awake.

'Time to rise and shine, Harriet,' she said, smiling down at me as she clipped me into my harness and attached the lead. 'You've got a big day ahead of you.'

EE frowned. 'Are you sure she can't escape from that? It doesn't look very tight.'

'She'll be fine, Dad. Harriet's a good girl these days, aren't you, Harriet?'

EE didn't look convinced, but then he caught sight of his watch. 'We'd better get a move on or we'll miss breakfast.'

He rubbed his hands together and licked his lips. 'I'm really looking forward to it.'

When the waitress arrived at our table with the food, I understood exactly why EE had been so eager to get down to the dining room. His plate was piled high with bacon, egg, sausages and beans and there was a glistening slice of fried bread on the side.

Susie shook her head, eyeing the bulge of his tummy under his shirt.

'You're supposed to be on a diet, Dad. Mum will be cross when she finds out you haven't stuck to it.'

EE tucked his napkin into his shirt and licked his lips. 'There's something you need to learn, Susie.' He paused to wave his fork at her. 'What happens on tour, stays on tour.'

'What does that mean?' Susie asked, with a puzzled look on her face, but I had a sneaky feeling I knew what he was getting at. Basically, he meant no telling tales about the tour once we were back at home.

EE pushed a forkful of food into his mouth. 'It means that diets are off the

58

menu,' he said, his voice muffled by bacon and beans. Then he swallowed and tapped the side of his nose in a secretive way. 'It means you keep mum to – er – Mum.'

While they carried on chatting, I looked around at the other guests. Over by the fresh fruit was an actress from a soap opera. I nibbled my carrot thoughtfully, should I wriggle out of my harness and pop over for a friendly chat? After my triumphant entrance the night before maybe I could give her some tips on wowing the paparazzi.

I looked at EE and Susie, they weren't paying me the slightest bit of attention.

Very carefully, I shuffled around in my seat, working the harness and lead over my shoulders. With another quick glance up to make sure no one was looking, I shook the harness off and hopped on to the floor.

Nose twitching, I set off towards the actress. From the smell of things, she was having apples and pears, my two favourite fruits. With a bit of luck she might be in the mood to share.

I was so busy drooling that I didn't pay much attention to where I was hopping. So I didn't see a waiter weaving towards me with a silver tray loaded with plates of all kinds of breakfast food. I might not even have noticed that I was next to Miranda and Doodle's table, if Doodle hadn't spotted me and lunged, her teeth bared in a threatening growl. I leaped sideways and her fangs missed my fur by centimetres.

The waiter wasn't so lucky. As Doodle turned her head for another snap, her mouth crunched on the poor man's leg.

'Ouch!' he yelped and threw his arms up in the air.

Doodle let go of his leg and looked innocently around. The tray spun, sending the plates somersaulting in one direction and the food in another. We all gazed upwards as, with a loud crash, the plates clattered into each other and fell to the floor. A second later, the food landed

too, but not on the rich red carpet. Instead, eggs and bacon splattered wetly on to the glossy head of the actress.

She let out a disgusted shriek. Holding his leg, the waiter yelled at Doodle. Miranda shouted at the waiter. Another waiter rushed over and began to pluck bits of egg out of the actress's hair.

In the midst of all the excitement, everyone seemed to have forgotten about me. Deciding it probably wasn't the best time to speak to the actress after all, I hot-footed it back to my table, where EE and Susie were craning their necks to see what the fuss was about.

'What's going on?' EE said, peering across the dining room.

'I don't know,' Susie replied. 'Something about a rabbit, I think.'

As one, they both turned to stare at my chair. I gazed back at them, nibbling at my carrot as though I'd been there the whole time.

'You don't think—' EE began, with a

suspicious look on his face.

Susie shook her head crossly. 'Honestly, Dad, you can't blame Harriet for everything. She hasn't moved from her seat!'

EE studied me for a moment, then blinked and shrugged. 'I suppose you're right. Now, how about a bowl of cornflakes?'

CHAPTER SEVEN
Twinkle, Twinkle, Superstar

I kept my head down during the briefing and spent most of it snuggled on Susie's lap, ignoring the evil looks that Miranda and Doodle were sending my way. Gloria did a lot of talking about where we had to be and when. EE stared at her like she was telling the most exciting story ever, nodding his head and clapping louder than anyone else at the end.

'Gery vood, Gloria,' he babbled, as she walked past us on the way out.

She flashed him a puzzled smile, then glanced down at me and Susie. 'All set for the dress rehearsal this afternoon, Harriet? I hope you've got some extra-special moves planned.'

I stood up on my back legs and waved my paws eagerly. I had lots of ideas for ways to wow the audience. Maybe you couldn't teach old dogs new tricks but Stunt Bunnies learned fast!

✦ ✦ ✦

The dress rehearsal went like a dream. Lulu the chimp hula-hooped like a tornado and the terrapins tumbled like never before. Even Doodle sounded *almost* in tune on the big stadium stage. Gloria seemed especially pleased with me.

'Simply marvellous, Harriet,' she said, beaming down at me. 'The crowd is going to go wild when they see your act.'

As Gloria walked away, Miranda glowered at us. She seemed to be in a very bad mood and refused to eat lunch with the rest of the owners.

'The chef has prepared a special meal for Doodle in her dressing room,' she announced, wrinkling her nose at the food laid out for everyone else. 'Singers have to watch what they eat. The tiniest crumb can affect their voices and she is the star of the show, after all.'

Wrapping a pink fluffy dressing gown around the poodle, Miranda whisked her away.

'Spike-tacular doesn't get special meals in their dressing room,' Sam said, glancing over at his hedgehogs chomping on vegetables in their cages. 'They don't even *have* a dressing room!'

The other owners grumbled in agreement.

'Doodle probably needs one so that no one has to hear her warm up,' EE joked.

Sam grinned. 'Maybe that's why Miranda is so cross. She should buy herself some earplugs.'

Everyone laughed except me. The problem was that Miranda thought Doodle was the best thing since sliced bread. She thought her poodle was the cat's whiskers, which only made me more determined to give one hundred and ten percent later. I'd show her who the star of *Superpets Live* really was!

✯ ✯ ✯

It was almost the end of the first show and Doodle had warbled her last wobbly note. As I hopped into the centre of the stage, an expectant hush descended over the crowd. I shook my sequinned suit and flicked my grey ears back and forth. This was it; the moment I loved the most. So they wanted to see Stunt Bunny, did they? Wait until they got a load of my latest tricks!

I started with a simple backflip, one kick of my powerful back legs sending me soaring into the air. Below me were four trampolines. I aimed for the one furthest away from me and hit it squarely in the middle. The audience gasped as I hurtled upwards and through a sparkling hoop high above the stage. This time I landed on

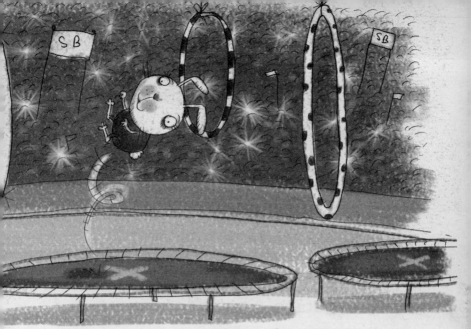

and spun towards another hoop hanging above the stage. Soon, I was bouncing between the trampolines and flying through the hoops, my sparkling costume making me look like a twinkling shooting star. The audience was whooping with delight.

After one final triple backflip, I landed on all fours on the stage, my ears quivering straight up in the air like an Olympic gymnast. The crowd erupted into thunderous cheers and some of them even got to their feet. Graciously, I tipped my head towards them.

'Way to go, Harriet,' Susie said, as I came off stage. She lifted me up and planted a big kiss on my velvety nose. 'You're definitely the star of the show!'

CHAPTER EIGHT
Mission Impossible

The next morning, we packed our bags and took the lift downstairs. The hotel lobby was busy with guests checking out. Susie and I picked our way through the piles of luggage to the waiting tour bus. EE puffed and panted behind us, loaded with my basket and bags.

'I thought there'd be people to carry this stuff for us,' he muttered under his breath as we joined the other pets and owners.

If EE thought I had a lot of luggage, he should see how much Doodle travelled with. Had I really just seen a set of hair curlers poking out of one of her cases?

Suddenly, a roadie appeared beside us. His lime-green baseball cap was pulled low over his bright red hair, hiding his face. 'Can I 'elp you, Signor Wilson?'

'Ah, excellent! You can take these, for a start,' EE said and he held the bags out to the roadie.

The man's eyes slid towards me. 'Of course. But first I take ze rabbit.'

'I beg your pardon?' EE said, lowering the bags in confusion. 'Take her where?'

'Zere ees a special car waiting for ze star of ze show,' the roadie said. 'She ees a VIP, no?'

I pictured a stretch limousine with carrot juice chilling inside and a 'BUNNY 1' number plate on the outside. It sounded great, but something was nagging at me – where had I heard that voice before? I twitched my nose, thinking hard. Maybe he worked at the *Superpets* studio.

EE tried to peer under the brim of the hat. 'Don't I know you from somewhere?'

The roadie lowered his head. 'I don't zeenk so, Signor Wilson.'

Frowning, EE tapped his cheek with one finger. 'I'm sure I've seen you before.' Then he shrugged and pointed at my basket. 'Never mind. In you go, Harriet.'

I hopped inside. EE hardly had time to fumble with the door clips before the roadie was swinging my basket into the air.

'See you soon, Harriet,' Susie called, disappearing on to the bus.

But, instead of heading towards a waiting limo, I found myself going back into the hotel lobby. I stared at the bus in confusion. Where exactly was this special car parked?

Miranda and Doodle passed us on their way to the bus. 'Have fun being a VIP,' Miranda cooed, wiggling her fingers at me. 'Missing you already!'

Miranda didn't seem at all surprised that I wasn't on the bus. And suddenly I started to panic, where on earth was the roadie taking me?

The roadie strode through the lobby

and into the crowded lift, just as the doors slid shut. Suddenly, I didn't believe I was heading for VIP treatment anymore. I was being bunny-napped!

'Top floor, pleeze,' I heard the roadie say and the lift flew upwards. *Ding!* The bell chimed as we passed the first floor. Whiskers twitching anxiously, I hoped one of the other passengers needed to

get out soon. If the lift went all the way to the top of the hotel, I stood no chance of catching the tour bus before it left.

I was in luck. On the third floor, the lift slowed down and the doors opened. The crowd shuffled to let the passengers out. Now was my chance! I nudged the door of my basket with my nose, hoping EE's clumsy fingers hadn't fastened the clips properly. *Yes!* The bottom of the door gave way and, quicker than you could say 'crinkly cabbage', I wriggled out of the basket, leaping towards the inviting blue carpet.

'*Oi!*' yelled the roadie, grabbing at my powder puff tail. He was too late. The lift doors were closing and once my paws made contact with the floor I was off, scampering towards the stairs, and freedom. But, when I reached them, I skidded to a halt. There were a *lot* of stairs and I didn't have much time. What I needed was a super speedy way of getting to the bottom.

Then I remembered what Sam had said about sliding down the stairs when we'd arrived at the hotel. It was perfect for a Stunt Bunny like me – I'd be on the ground floor in no time!

I jumped up on to the banister and ears flat, I crouched low and whizzed round the corkscrew curves. As the hotel lobby zoomed into sight, I looked up. The tour bus was still there! With a giant thrust, I pushed off the banister with my back feet, flying through the air into the lobby.

Seconds later, I was racing across the floor, zipping through legs and hopping over the piles of suitcases. The revolving door spun as I shot out the other side. Then I was on the red carpet, but I could see the doors of the bus starting to close. With another giant final leap, I twisted sideways with my paws outstretched, closing my eyes and hoping I'd make it through the narrowing gap.

'Harriet!' cried Susie as the door hissed shut and I landed on the top step next to the driver. 'Why aren't you in your special car?'

She rushed to the front of the bus and gathered me up. Miranda and Doodle swapped disappointed glances as Susie fussed over me. Somehow, I knew they'd been behind my attempted bunny-napping, but they were no match for a Stunt Bunny.

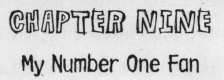

CHAPTER NINE

My Number One Fan

EE grumbled about having to buy a new travel basket to replace the one I'd escaped from, but he didn't have much choice, although he did make sure he bought a practically escape-proof basket this time. The rest of the tour went in a blur. Up and down Britain we went, amazing the audience in Manchester, flabbergasting the fans in Birmingham and crazing the crowds in Cardiff. Our final show was London, and Gloria warned us to expect our biggest audience ever.

'Pull out all the stops, gang!' she urged at our pre-show pep talk. 'Doodle, hit those high notes. Lulu, spin it like you've never spun before. And Harriet—' she paused and beamed at me. 'You don't need to change a thing.'

It was a proud moment. Susie tickled my cheek fondly and even EE seemed to be glad he was sitting next to me. Doodle, on the other hand, looked like someone had done a poo under her nose.

'Don't forget Mum and Lily are coming to see the show tonight, Harriet,' Susie whispered. 'Make sure you give them a wave.'

As if she needed to remind me. I'd give the performance of my life that night or my name wasn't Harriet Houdini!

✫ ✫ ✫

There was a crowd waiting when we arrived at the stadium. They cheered as we got off the bus and cameras flashed all around us. Then a sudden shriek split the air. 'Harriet! Harriet Houdini!'

Rushing towards us was a girl around Susie's age, wearing pink and white flashing bunny ears and an 'I ♥ Stunt Bunny!' T-shirt. Behind her was a harassed looking security guard. The girl skidded to a halt in front of us, ears wobbling. 'Is it really you?'

'Who else would it be?' Miranda drawled, as she waved her hand in a big fake yawn.

Susie smiled at the girl. 'That's right. Would you like an autograph?'

Wide-eyed, the girl nodded. 'I'm Stunt Bunny's number one fan!'

I busied myself putting my paw print on to a photograph as the girl chattered away. I barely noticed Miranda disappear back on to the bus. By the time I'd

finished with my super-fan and the guard had taken her back to her mother, EE had decided I'd be safer in my basket and he climbed aboard the bus to get it.

'Where's Harriet's water bottle gone?' Susie exclaimed when he placed it on the floor beside us. 'It was attached to her basket when we set off.'

Now, don't get me wrong, I'm not the

kind of VIP who demands white roses from Paris or the hottest hairdresser, but a girl gets used to having her own things around and my water bottle was one of them. Apart from anything else, I'd nibbled the nozzle into just the right shape for drinking from.

'Perhaps it fell off during the journey,' EE said doubtfully.

'Looking for something?' Miranda popped up next to us. She was smiling.

'Harriet's water bottle has gone missing,' EE said.

'Is this it?' Miranda asked, holding something towards us. 'I found it rolling around the floor of the bus.'

'That's it!' Susie exclaimed. 'Look, Harriet, it's your water bottle.'

As pleased as I was to see it, I couldn't shake my feeling of distrust. Miranda was never helpful unless there was something in it for her. I stared at Doodle, trying to work out what the two of them were planning. Doodle stared back, her teeth bared in a friendly grin.

Susie took the bottle. 'If it's been on the floor I'd better give it a wash.'

'No need!' trilled Miranda, quick as a flash. 'I already did that for you.'

Now I was definitely suspicious. Something was up. But Susie and EE didn't seem to have noticed.

'Thanks, Miranda,' EE said with a grateful smile. 'I don't know what we'd have done if you hadn't found it.'

Susie clipped the bottle back on to my basket and carried me through the entrance to the hotel. Peering over my shoulder, I saw Miranda and Doodle high five behind us. I didn't know what they were up to, but I was ready. If they thought I was even *sniffing* that bottle, they had another thing coming.

CHAPTER TEN
Backstage Surprises

The dress rehearsal was a disaster. Spike-tacular fell in a heap, Lulu dropped her hula hoop and there were problems with the stage lights, which caused Gloria to rush around with a stressed look on her face, shouting a lot. By the time we'd finished everyone was feeling frazzled.

'I don't know about you, Harriet, but I'll be glad when the show is over tonight,' the make-up lady said, as she put the finishing touches to my hair and whiskers. 'What with all the problems today and that awful singing, I'm looking forward to a nice rest.'

A pained look crossed her face and I knew she meant Doodle, who we could hear warming up somewhere backstage. For an opera-singing poodle, some of those notes sounded a bit wobbly. But, now I came to think about it, I was looking forward to going home after the show too. My hutch was 'cosy', but at least I didn't have to listen to EE snoring all night.

✤ ✤ ✤

Susie and EE had gone to collect Mrs Wilson and Lily from the train station, so once I'd finished in make-up I had nothing to do but wait for them to get back. Most of the other pets were in their dressing rooms, so it was all quiet in the area behind the stage. As I sat there, snacking on some hay, I heard a sharp whisper behind the dark backstage curtains. I stopped chewing to listen.

'Pssst! Are you 'ere?'

I frowned. That funny accent was

familiar. Where had I heard it before?

A snooty female voice whispered back, 'Of course I am. Did you bring the lookalike?'

My frown got deeper. I'd know that toffee-nosed tone anywhere. But who earth was Miranda whispering to?

'I 'ave,' the other voice replied. "Ave you given 'Arriet ze sleeping potion?'

Eyes wide, I shuffled to the front of my basket and peered out, but there was no one to be seen.

'It's in the water bottle. Her stupid owners didn't suspect a thing.'

I stared at the bottle, hanging from my door. So that was why it had gone missing – Miranda must have taken it!

'Good. Once she is asleeps, I will swap 'er for ze – 'ow you say – look-ze-samey.'

'It's called a lookalike, you idiot,' Miranda said. 'Just make sure you take the right rabbit away. When Gloria sees her precious Stunt Bunny has forgotten how to backflip, she'll kick her off *Superpets* and beg Doodle to take her place!'

So that was it! Miranda wanted Doodle to be the star of *Superpets* and she didn't care what it took. But who was her partner in crime?

Wriggling to the back of my basket, I considered my options. What I needed was a way out of the basket so I could get help, but the basket that EE had bought made sure I had little chance of escaping. I could only hope that Susie and EE came back before Miranda and the mystery man could put their dastardly plan into practice.

The backstage curtains twitched and a dark figure came towards me. Quick as a flash, I lay flat on the floor of the basket and narrowed my eyes to slits. If the man thought I was asleep I might be able to catch him by surprise and hop away to safety when he opened the door. But the mystery man didn't open the basket. Instead, he bent down to look inside.

'Allo 'Arriet,' he said. 'We meet again.'
I peered out and was shocked to find
myself face to face with the only person
that could possibly spell more trouble
for me than Doodle's owner...

'Don't worry, Miranda.' He called, 'Zis
time, I, ze Great Maldini, will not fail. I
must 'ave zis rabbit!'

CHAPTER ELEVEN

Stunt Double

I don't mind telling you that my heart was pounding. The last time I'd seen the Great Maldini, he'd tried to steal me away to star in his magic show. Only a super bunny backflip had saved me and now it looked as though he was trying again. But how had he got past the security guards and into the stadium?

As I looked more closely at Maldini, suddenly it became clear how he had managed to get backstage. Gone was the dark hair he'd had when I'd last seen him. Instead, on his head was a red wig, covered by a familiar lime-green baseball cap. The Great Maldini and the kidnapping roadie were the same person!

He lifted his hand and I saw he held a travel basket identical to mine. Sitting in the middle was a grey rabbit. It looked exactly like me!

''Arriet 'Oudini, meet 'Arriet 'Oudini,' the Great Maldini said and started to giggle. 'By ze time everyone works out what 'as 'appened, we will be far away.'

Still laughing, he raised my basket up in the air and swung the other basket into its place. Then, with a flourish, he shook out a black cloth and draped it over my basket. Everything went dark.

My main worry was that he would whisk me away immediately, but I could still hear Doodle's awful singing when he put me down again, so I knew we hadn't gone far.

'Wait 'ere, my little Stunt Bunny,' he said, whipping away the cloth and grinning evilly. 'When I return, we escapes!'

He tugged something over the front

of my basket and I was in the dark again. Gnashing my teeth together, I thought hard. From the sounds of things, he'd hidden me away somewhere backstage. But when Susie and EE came back, they would see the lookalike rabbit and think it was me!

By the time they realised their mistake The Great Maldini would be long gone, taking me with him. I needed to hatch a getaway plan, and fast. But what could I do? The basket was escape-proof. Or was it?

I nibbled at the plastic wall beside me, but it was tough and hurt my teeth. The door of the basket was no better. It looked like plastic, until I clamped my trusty teeth on it and discovered it was made of metal coated with plastic.

Then I heard something which made me want to cry. Susie had come back and she'd gone straight to the lookalike bunny's basket.

'Sorry we were gone so long, Harriet,' I heard her say. 'Dad got lost.'

'I did not,' EE sounded snappy. 'Your mother gave me the wrong directions.'

The backstage speaker crackled and a voice said, 'Ten minutes to curtain up. All pets to the stage.'

'You'd better get Harriet dressed,' EE said. 'She's on in a minute.'

I peered frantically around my dark prison, searching for a way out. There wasn't one and with all the noise from the other pets heading towards the stage, no-one could hear my squeaking.

'Has Harriet lost weight?' Susie said slowly. 'Only this sparkly suit fitted her

107

yesterday and now it's too big.'

I froze, hoping Susie would realise that the rabbit she held wasn't me, but EE growled impatiently, 'Just put it on and let's get on stage. The curtain will go up in a minute and Gloria won't be pleased if we're not there.'

Seconds later, they were gone. In desperation, I kicked out at the wall of the basket, but it was designed to stand up to bigger bunnies than me and didn't budge. Defeated, I stared up at the roof. And then it hit me. There was a hatch in the roof big enough for Susie to slide her hand through. It had a latch to hold it closed, but maybe if I could hit it with my back feet I could get it open! The question was, how was I going to reach the roof?

CHAPTER TWELVE

There's only one Stunt Bunny!

Applause and cheering floated through from the stage, meaning the show had started. I guessed it wouldn't be long before the Great Maldini came back. If I didn't act fast, I'd never see Susie again! Waggling my whiskers, I thought hard. The roof was too low for a backflip and

I didn't fancy bumping my head if I jumped. But, if I balanced on my front paws, maybe I could kick upwards and break-out.

Taking a deep breath, I planted my paws in front of me and did a handstand. Then, with one powerful thump, I hit out at the roof of the cage and caught the hatch with a terrific thrust. The latch snapped and I felt the hatch fly upwards. Quickly, I stood on all fours and nudged at the broken roof. The gap was just big enough for me to jump through. I slid to the floor. Now to get to the stage and show them who the real Stunt Bunny was around here!

'Not so fast, 'Arriet!' cried a voice above me.

I looked up to see the Great Maldini coming towards me, an evil sneer on his face. 'So you zeenk you can escape, no? I 'ave news for you – no one escapes ze Great Maldini!'

Except me, of course. As his hands reached out to grab me, I set off along the ground at top speed. I'd been right when I'd guessed he hadn't taken me far. In fact, he'd hidden my basket under the make-up lady's table. With a howl, Maldini lunged after me, his hands grabbing and missing as I zig-zagged across the floor. In the background,

I could hear Doodle's warbling yowls, which meant it was almost time for my act. I had to hurry if I wanted to save the show.

The Great Maldini was puffing and panting as he chased me. I stopped zig-zagging from side to side and began circling around him. His fingers snatched at my fur as he spun, missing

me by inches each time. He turned round faster and faster and let out a dizzy-sounding groan. Then he lurched off to one side, clutching his head.

'I spin like ze fairground tea-cups,' he moaned. 'Make eet stop!'

I didn't have time feel sorry for him – the applause for Doodle's performance was fading and a hush had settled over the crowd. I needed to get to the stage before the lookalike rabbit ruined my reputation forever.

With a giant leap, I cleared the steps to the stage and bounded into the bright lights, where everyone was staring at the pretend me cowering on one of trampolines.

'Go on, Harriet,' Susie whispered uncertainly, from the side of the stage. 'People are waiting. Do a backflip or something.'

You could have heard a pin drop in the silence. The other rabbit gazed back at Susie with big eyes, her ears twitching nervously. Slowly, I hopped into the centre of the stage. The audience gasped

when they saw me and Susie's mouth dropped open in shock. 'Harriet?'

On the other side of the stage, I noticed Miranda go a peculiar colour. She began to tug Doodle backwards.

Gloria pushed to the front of the stage. 'Surely the rabbit on the trampoline is the real Harriet?' she said, glancing between the lookalike bunny and me in confusion.

Suddenly, everyone was talking at once and the crowd was joining in too.

'I suppose there's only one way to be sure,' Susie said, lifting me on to a trampoline. 'Go on, Harriet.' She looked at the other rabbit. 'Or . . . erm . . . Harriet.'

116

The lookalike squeaked and leaped sideways, but I didn't need to be told twice. Pushing off against the trampoline, I was soon soaring high above the stage. Cheers broke out around the stadium as I spun through the hoops and bouncing between the trampolines. The crowd went wild when I finally pulled off a perfect triple flip and landed beside Susie.

Gloria lifted the microphone to her mouth and smiled. 'I don't think there's any doubt about who the real Harriet Houdini is, do you?' she said over the cheers. 'There's only one Stunt Bunny!'

CHAPTER THIRTEEN

There's no place like home

By the time the audience had finished applauding and we got off the stage, there was no sign of Maldini, apart from his baseball cap and wig.

'Didn't these belong to that roadie?' EE said, picking them up from the floor and frowning at them. 'You know, I wouldn't be surprised if he had something to do with all this.'

Gloria looked confused. 'But we don't have a roadie with red hair.'

Everyone stared at the wig in EE's hands.

'Is that the time?' Miranda burst out in a bright voice. 'Gosh, we really must be going. Come along, Doodle!'

And tugging on the poodle's lead, the two of them disappeared out of the door before anyone could stop them. I decided it was best to let them go. Miranda had failed in her attempt to get me thrown off *Superpets* and there was no way I could prove she'd even tried.

'There's something very strange about

those two,' EE said, staring after them.

At that moment the door flew open again and Mrs Wilson and Lily burst through. Mrs Wilson gave Susie a big hug and Lily gave me a sticky hug.

1, 2, 3, 4

'What on earth was all that about?' she asked curiously. 'Where did that other rabbit come from?'

'No idea,' EE said. 'But it definitely isn't ours.'

That raised another question. What was going to happen to the lookalike rabbit now that The Great Maldini had fled?

'You can be my bunny,' Lily said, putting me down to pick up the grey rabbit and rubbing her face against its soft fur. 'I will call you Flopsy.'

'No!' chorused Susie, EE and Mrs Wilson all at the same time.

'That's what we called Harriet when we first got her,' EE went on with a shudder. 'And we can't keep this rabbit, Lily. One bunny is quite enough.'

'I've always wanted a pet of my own,' Gloria said thoughtfully, reaching across to lift the rabbit out of Lily's arms. 'Maybe I can give Flopsy a home.'

She stroked Flopsy under her chin and the bunny closed her eyes happily. She didn't even seem to mind her new name. What can I say? It takes all sorts.

'G-g-great idea,' EE stuttered, looking a bit like he wanted Gloria to tickle him under the chin.

Mrs Wilson threw him a frosty look. 'I see you're still ga-ga.' EE went red. 'I don't know what you mean.'

'Hmmmmm,' Mrs Wilson said, raising an eyebrow. 'Susie and I need to have a long chat about exactly what's been going on.'

Susie dropped me a great

big wink. 'Oh, you know what they say, Mum. What happens on tour, stays on tour!'

She wouldn't get any arguments from me. The sooner I forgot about The Great Maldini again, the better. EE seemed to agree too.

'I've been thinking about Harriet's hutch,' he said as we walked towards the exit. 'Maybe we'll see if the pet shop has a Mulberry Mansion in stock now.'

Susie squealed with delight, but she wasn't as pleased as I was. I'd been looking forward to getting back to my own hutch and now that I knew I was getting an upgrade, I was even keener.

Being a Stunt Bunny on tour was all very well, but there really was no place like home.

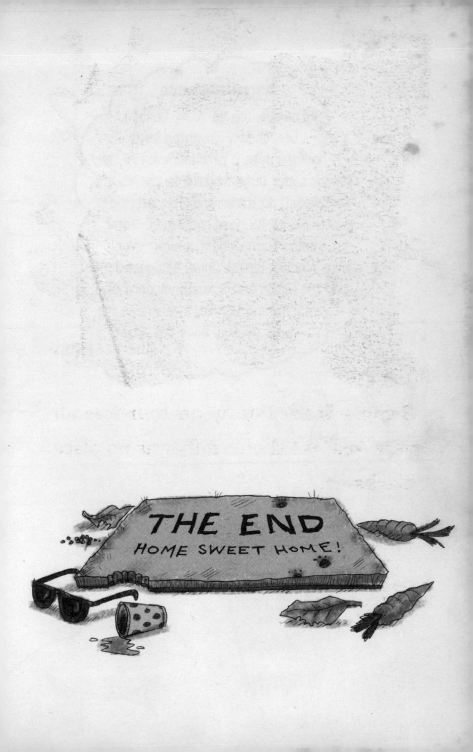

Acknowledgements

As always, big up to my husband,
Lee, and my daughter, Tania;
no more pets, I promise, even if they
do look super cute. Thanks to the World's
Best Agent, Jo Williamson, for putting
up with me, to Richard and Janice Slater,
for being the loveliest in-laws ever,
and to Venetia, Editor Jane, Designer Jane
and the Simon and Schuster superstars,
for making Harriet's journey
a lot of fun. Rock on!